THE SCARED ONE

THE SCARED ONE

Written by Dennis Haseley   Drawings by Deborah Howland

FREDERICK WARNE   NEW YORK   LONDON

LIBRARY OF CONGRESS CATALOGING IN PUBLICATION DATA
Haseley, Dennis. The scared one.
SUMMARY: A young Indian boy is called the scared one until
he gains strength and courage from an injured bird he has rescued.
[1. Courage—Fiction. 2. Indians of North America—Fiction.
3. Birds—Fiction] I. Howland, Deborah, ill. II. Title.
PZ7.H2688Sc 1983   [E]   82-20109
ISBN 0-7232-6185-7

FREDERICK WARNE & CO., INC. NEW YORK, NEW YORK

Printed in the U.S.A. by The Murray Printing Co.

Book design by Barbara DuPree Knowles

1 2 3 4 5 87 86 85 84 83

For my mother — D. HASELEY

For my children Megan and Ariel — D. HOWLAND

They call me the Scared One
because I run from things,
because I am afraid
of the night
and the big dogs
even when those in our village
who are smaller than me
are not afraid.
And anyone can call me
the Scared One.
Anyone can say
what they like about me
and I will stay and smile,
for the others know
I am most afraid
of being alone.

And in the school they told us
that my tribe was once proud
although today
only a few old people
know the language.
And they said that once
a young man of this tribe
would go to a wild place
by himself,
would go without his food,
without his sleep,
until an animal
came to him
in a dream
to be his guide
for all his life . . .

and in the classroom
I closed my eyes
and tried to see
the animal that would
come for me—
a bear
or a deer—
and the boys laughed
when they saw me
and told the teacher
I was dreaming
of a little mouse.

And that night at the table
my mother looked at me
for a long time,
and then she asked
if I would like to talk.
I shook my head.
"I understand," she said.
"You are almost a man."
I nodded, then I
walked from the room
quickly so she would not see
and put my face down
on my cot
and my tears flowed
from my little mouse heart.

I slept then,
but it was during the night
that our goat
chewed through his rope,
and in my dream
of running from my village
I heard his bell
grow softer
and softer.

And in the morning
my mother gave me
a piece of jerky
and a rope
and sent me off
through the fields
all alone
running to keep up
with my heart.

My house grew so small
a crow could pluck it.
My house!

And when I was so far away
and alone
I lay by a rock . . . .

And when I looked up again
I saw the clear sky
begin to fill . . .
first one cloud
and then another,
and I watched and
felt afraid and
they came faster. They
swarmed dark and thick
like the buffaloes in the hunt
we read about,
buffaloes, with horses
charging, the wind
howling like my ancestors,
the lightning flashing
like their arrows!
And before I could think,
before I could remember
I was afraid,
I stood and gave a yell
for I seemed to see
a flash of blood
in that sky!
And then the thunder
knocked me from my feet
and I remembered
nothing.

After a time
the sun grew warm
on my back
and I woke
and saw the goat
nuzzling the grass.
I reached and
grabbed his rope . . .
and then I saw the bird!

He stood near me
with his wings stretched
the length of my arms
and they were bright, like flames,
and his eyes stared into mine.

I sat up slowly
but he did not move.
"Go," I said. "Fly." And he
tilted his head.
Then I saw the crook
in his wing
like a twig
broken by a storm.
"You can't fly," I said,
and his eyes seemed
to know my words.
I took my shirt—
my heart was beating
like a caught bird—
and I put it
over his folded wings,
and then I lifted him gently.
He was light.

And then the goat
and the bird
and I
went through the fields
toward my village.

When we returned
it was night
and I tied the goat
and went into my house.
My mother was cooking
and I lifted the shirt
and she turned and looked at me
a long time.
"You cannot keep him,"
she said. "He will die here."
I looked down.
His eyes were closed,
and I felt afraid.
"If you want to help him," she said,
and her voice was soft
like it had not been for a long time,
"then you must take him
to Old Wolf. He
knows of such things."

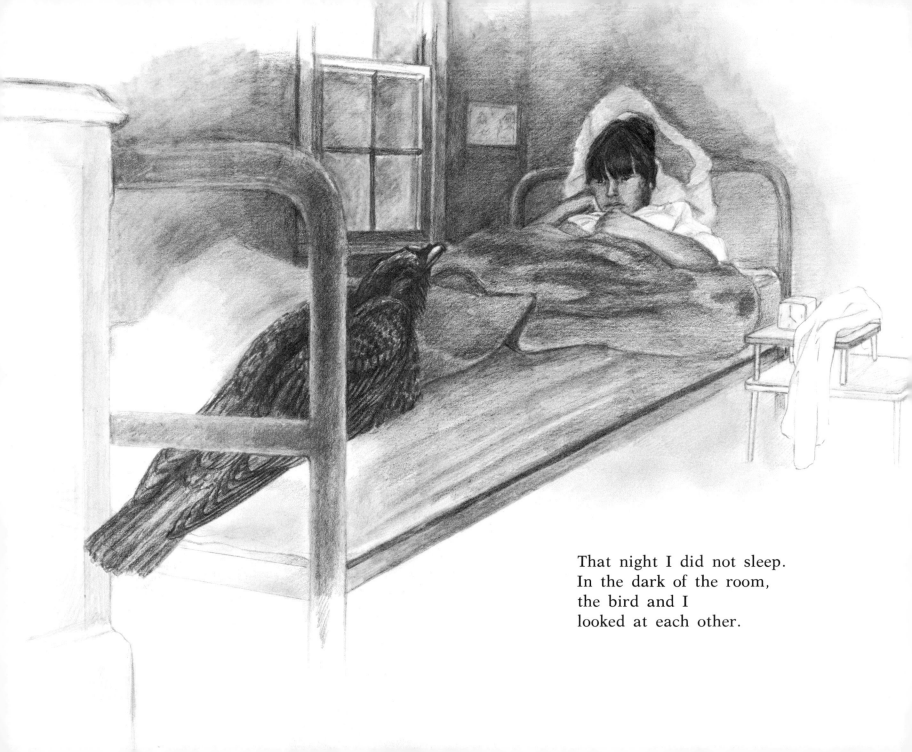

That night I did not sleep.
In the dark of the room,
the bird and I
looked at each other.

And at the first light
I wrapped him in my shirt
and walked through the village
while the families were eating,
and the boys came to their windows
and called out to me:
"Hey, Scared One, mouse,
where are you going?"
And I nodded and smiled,
though I did not want to,
and walked up the road,
alone,
to the dwelling of the man
who would help my bird fly.
He was a member of the tribe
though now he lived by the highway
and sold things to the visitors
who came to see the village.

When I got to the door
of his trailer
it seemed like he was
waiting for me.

I spoke fast like a rabbit.
"I have a bird that is sick.
I was told you could heal him."
He looked at me and did not smile.
Then he said for me
to show him the bird.
When I lifted the shirt
his eyes opened wide.
"This bird is very sick," he said.
"I will do what I can.
You go home, now."

I gave him my bird,
but when I turned to go
my heart felt sick
though I did not know why.
Then I heard a
flapping of wings,
and I turned and saw
Old Wolf holding on to my bird
while the bird beat his wings.
But when my bird
saw me
he stopped
and tilted his head.
And it was as if
everything slowed down.

I looked around
the walls of the trailer . . .
and saw the broken arrows,
the chipped flints
of warriors,
the rusted knives
beneath the glass.
And along the walls
on perches
I saw the birds,

frozen there,
with their wings spread,
who would stay and never fly,
and I saw how
my own bird might look,
frozen, never moving,
his eyes replaced with glass,
his legs on a metal stand,
a tag on his neck,
and oh, I wished to see him fly!

Then I grew very still
while something in my chest
began to beat,
strong and steady,
trying to get out,
and I said, "No,"
sharply, and I took my bird
and I turned
and ran from his trailer,
and I could hear Old Wolf
shouting
in the language of my ancestors.

And when I reached the road
I saw
the boys from my village
waiting for me
and they were not smiling.
"Give us what you have," they said.
"Give us what is in the shirt."
I looked at them as
they walked toward me,

and I felt the beating
in my chest,
and I took my bird
from my shirt
and he leapt
onto my arm,
my bare arm,
and he clutched there
with his claws,
and the boys stood back,
and then, oh,
I raised him
and the words came from inside.
"*WaNyaka Michante!*
Behold my heart!
WaNyaka Mi wowaske!
Behold my strength!"
And how the sun was rising,
and he stretched out his wings
his flashing wings,
his wings of flame
and I said, "You must fly now,"
and he clutched my arm
and like my own fire
my blood ran!

"*Kinan Po!* Fly now!" I cried.
"*Ake Akisne!*
You must grow strong
while you fly!"
And I thrust my arm
into the air . . .
He tilted his head
at me. He looked
into my eyes . . .

and he turned
and rose
and, oh, I could feel his wings
beating in my chest
and I cried
"I will never fear!
I will never die!"
And he rose
into the flame of the sky
into the blood of my life!